HEART WAR

A COLLECTION OF HEARTFUL LOVE STORIES

SUNEEL GEE

To my family the basis of my existence

Contents

Preface

This is an assembling of my understanding of the emotion called love, nothing more and nothing less.

ONE
LOVE LETTER

In the Year 1998, Somewhere around Nepal

Dipak is hiding under the yellow mustard field spread over infinity, even an eagle's gaze would find it hard to locate the nearby houses. He is wearing plain blue school attire with dark trousers, his books are scattered on the ground. Sun is about to drown below the mountains and flocks of birds flying in rhythm, signaling, they are homebound. He is gasping for breath, his red tomato face sweating profusely and his feet trembling with a colossal struggle to support his wobbly body. Dipak's eyes are fixed upon the narrow path ahead lined up with the parade of trees, his dark pupils bursting with anxiety and restlessness. It seems he is waiting for someone with bated breath. A young girl enters the scene; she is walking timidly with school books tucked to her chest through that narrow isolated path. A gentle breeze of summer breezes past Dipak, like a hearty welcome of her belated arrival, those yellow mustard petals are dancing with the wind. His both arms sweep across those jigging petals, he moves ahead cautiously and stretches his giraffe-like long neck. That girl pauses her movement, she looks around, Dipak swiftly sinks below the flowers. She has a symmetrical face with hair tied by a red ribbon, the most notable feature is her sharp focused nose. Convinced there is no one around, she opens the book and extracts a piece of paper. Dipak again stretches his neck, carefully and immaculately concealing his presence. The twilight sun illuminates upon her face; her dark eyes glitter, she starts reading the content of the paper. Dipak swallowing his saliva clasps his chest realizing his palpitation is escalating rapidly. His face turned intense red and the flow of sweats was abundant. She is reading the paper, *that's what her focused eyes and murmuring lips seem to convey*. Due to the considerable distance, he is struggling to analyze her expression. Dipak makes a desperate move to get closer but the girl swiftly tucks that piece of paper inside the book again and starts walking away. His heart skips a beat; wobbly feet fail as his body plunges to the ground. He whimpers, his gaze collects the last glimpse of her vanishing in the narrow path. Dipak's whole existence is trampling the mustard flower, *his oblivious gaze turns towards the cloudless blue sky, flawlessly blue, calm, still, and silent in complete contrast to his sorry situation.*

Her name is *Dipika,* both were in the same class from the only school in the sleepy town. Dipak and Dipika, identical names with not-so-identical academic performance though. Dipika is a class topper and Dipak is a below-average student. Dipika had this aura, the entourage of admirers followed her, and *Dipak nobody gave a shit about him,* like furniture in a room hardly ever noticed. Their name though was the tie binding their existence together, like the catalyst of their unnamed, incomprehensible relationship. They were relentlessly teased by their classmates, with several instances where the blackboard was always scribbled with the name *Dipak + Dipika*. Dipika always maintained her cool, nor did she blush nor was she embarrassed, silently ignored the commotion, and erased those words before the arrival of the class teacher. But it was Dipak who yelled and roared to keep their mouth shut, always infuriated with their antics, he harbored no sort of feelings nor any intentions of acquainting with Dipika, just loathed and cursed his own name. His best friend *Adarsha* always recited recurring advice *"You are too dumbass my friend, marry Dipika and you may have a bright future."* And Dipak's reply *"Worry about your own future smartass."* The irony Adarsha was equally weak in studies, tagged a monkey, his uneven hairy face reminded of one, full of mischief and the record holder of receiving teacher's punishment, the permanent mark of the teacher's cane on his posterior validated it.

"Love is like whisk of air, without any slightest of hints it breezes past you and your soul stirs in its flow." Love happened, one fine morning of Dashain's vacation, he woke up with the image of Dipika hovering around in his thought's orbit. *The moment where Dipika is gracefully erasing their names on the blackboard, the fragment of the white dust flowing in the air and traveling towards his nostrils. Her hair was tied with red ribbon, that sharply focused nose, and her unfathomable stoic face.* She is so mysterious; this was her first impression. His body temperature soared and his throat dried, Dipak flinched out of the room and he ran a mile. Nothing changed, her image in his mind intact except for every part of his pore body showered with sweats. Heturned ballistic with the question, *what is happening to me?* Mutton rice tasted like rubber, sleep distanced away, zero focus literally zero, days passed away with her image delving deeper into his consciousness. Failing to contain his emotions, Dipak understood it is love, what else could it be? And he

confessed about the turn of events to who else? *His best friend Adarsha.* But he burst out laughing, Adarsha giggled and ridiculed his friend's declaration.

"Are you only going to laugh?" Dipak complained.

Adarsha jumped on his bed and laughed more loudly. Dipak is left fuming.

"Write a love letter and give it to her on the first day of school," Adarsha suggested after a prolonged period of a hearty laugh.

"What?" Dipak's voice cracked.

"Yes dumbass."

"But... what if she rejects me like other boys?"

"You know; I am also hoping for a hard slap." Adarsha chuckled and exhibited that yellow stained teeth.

Dipak sighed deeply.

"That's my advice, take it or leave it,"Adarsha claimed boastfully.

"Aren't there any better ideas to tackle this?" Dipak asked.

"You like Dipika and it is the only solution." Adarsha chewed the *Pan Parag* stolen from his father's pocket.

Dipak leaned his heavy head and stepped out of the room on a dejected note.

"Wait.", Adarsha called him.

Dipak turned back.

"I am not sure about this but last year when you won the running competition." Adarsha paused.

"And?" Dipak asked with eyes wide open.

"And you were awarded RS 50 by Ramesh sir and the whole class was cheering your name."

"And?"

"In the crowd, I think I saw," Adarsha scratched his thick curly hair.

"What did you see?" Dipak's arm grabbed his collar.

"I am not sure though." Adarsha lingered over the revelation.

"What did you see?" Dipak's grip tightened over his collar.

"I think I saw Dipika smile." Adarsha struggled to speak.

"So?" Dipak released his grip.

"So, Dipika only smiles the day, every one commemorates her for excelling in exam."

Dipak tugged his hair in confusion.

"Dumbass, Dipika's smile is an event in itself like a full moon night."

"Yes." Dipak finally grasped his friend's point.

Adarsha shook his head in disbelief.

"Don't get your hopes up, you know my vision is weak."

"Thanks." Dipak smiled, hugged, and sprinted outside.

"Girls like poems," Adarsha yelled.

Love transcends time and logic, with that sudden sprout of confidence, Dipak wrote a love letter. It started with a short poem, though its authenticity was questionable.

This is not for fun
Don't tell your mom
My feelings are sincere
With a message to share
I wish someday you won't erase
Those letters on the blackboard scribbled with our name

My question to you is, "Did you really smile when I won that running competition last year?"

Though the writing can hardly be considered a love letter,Dipak murmured *"Poem writing is not that hard eh..."* He tucked it inside the pillow and desperately waited for the school to open. And that day came, as the final bell rang signaling the end of school, it was time for the ultimate test. In the isolated path, Dipak and Adarsha waited for her arrival, they both read the letter one last time.

"Can't believe even you could write a poem like this. God.... love is powerful." Adarsha confessed staring at the sky.

Dipak quietly tucked it inside his pocket with a deep sigh. The footstep is heard; Dipika arrived, welcomed by the gentle breeze of wind and dancing paddy fields. Dipak went numb, his sensory organs stopped functioning. She paused her steps finding both of the guys in the way. Dipak turned toward Adarsha with a panic-stricken face.

"All the best." Adarsha escaped from the scene like a sly fox.

"Coward." Dipak cursed his friend.

He turned back, both stood parallel, nowhere to hide, no fear of the classmates, nothing. Fear struck, his feet moved on their own and closed the distance. Now only inches apart, he listened to her breathing, his nostril tasted the sweet scent of her hair. He gazed at her silent red lips but dared not to raise his chin. *Eye contact, that could had resulted in the apocalypse, swift obliteration of his existence into a speck of dust.* His shivering arm forwarded the piece of paper. As Dipika clutched it in her palms, he ran away like a wind leaving an aftermath of fluttered dust in the air and hid under that spacious mustard field. *And the rest is history.*

Dipak wakes up from the flashback, it is about to get dark, and he stands up leaving a trail of crippled mustard flowers and leaves carrying a heavy heart. *What will be her reply? Her answer? Do I even stand a chance?* A burning question raging inside him, he felt he has grown older by a decade. The only silver lining or so-called hope was Dipika didn't tear apart the love letter like the way she had broken million hearts of schoolboys in the past. He skips dinner that night and a recurring dream of Dipika's powerful slap in front of the whole class bugs his whole night. He wakes up with a fever, a kind of fever where his heart is blazing with soaring temperature, burdened with the insurmountable weight wait of her reply. He collects a cassette album of Narayan Gopal from his father's room, affirming the *"Malai Nasodha"* song will be his anthem and a counselor in case of heartbreak. He heads off to school preparing for the humiliation and the ultimate rejection. On the way, he meets as usual his best friend Adarsha.

"You left me all alone, you chickened out," Dipak complains.

"Yes I did," Adarsha pauses, "Tell me what happened yesterday?" Adarsha grabs his cheeks and inspects them.

"What are you doing?" Dipak shoves him away.

"I am checking if there is any mark of Dipika's slap."

"Shut up, nothing happened, I just gave her the letter and ran away."

"That's it?"

"Yes I hid below the field to check up on her reaction but she just read the letter and walked away," Dipak confesses.

"She is so mysterious."

"Yes, she is." Dipak agrees.

"Hum...." Adarsha thinks for a bit, "Coming to think of it, I admire your courage bro."

"Really?"

"Yes starting from today I won't call you dumbass."

They both reach the class only to find out Dipika has yet to arrive. Dipak takes a sigh of relief. As the class is carrying on, Dipika enters the classroom late. She has a glint in her eyes, her face is looking fresh as the first day of spring, unadulterated and crude. Dipak finds her more beautiful and alluring.

"You are gone my friend; she will humiliate you in front of the whole class." Adarsha warns him.

Dipak gulps down his saliva. With the conclusion of every class, with every alarming bell, his paranoia grows with the thought of Dipika tearing apart the love letter in front of the whole class, the sky will fall upon him, the floor will collapse and he falls into a dark abyss. But nothing sort of that manifested, she is her usual self, timid yet attentive.

"No sort of any reaction till now?" Deepak questions Adarsha chewing the fistful of WaiWai noodle.

"Yes, what could be in her mind?" Adarsha escalates the curiosity.

"What should I do?" Deepak scratches his hair in despair.

"Wait." Adarsha inserts his hand into his pocket.

Dipak stares at him in confusion.

"Have this," Adarsha offers him a Mango Frooti, "I know you are tensed, thought this sweet drink will calm you down."

Dipak smiles and wraps his arms around Adarsha's shoulder.

Since the start of the last period, it started raining and still pouring without any sign of slowing down. No one dared to exit the shelter of the school, that merciless rain is intimidating and inviting at the same time. But the group of boys choose the latter, they grab a football and rush outside for fun.

"Let's go Dipak," Adarsha calls him.

Dipak turns towards Dipika, she is on her seat engrossed in books. His fatigued mind and body desperately demanded rest but before he can make a call, Adarsha pulls his collar and now they are tussling on the ground. The group of 6 boys starts playing football in the slippery mud-filled playground. Rain is punishing and drenching every pore of his body but he is now engrossed in this adrenaline pump, shaking off the weight of his emotions. The constant tussle for the ball, frequent tumbling on the ground, the invigorating sensation of the raindrops, everything felt so liberating, he is feeling his 16-year-old self again. Out of nowhere the ball smashes into his face, Dipak trips to the ground, temporally blinded by the pain and onslaught of rain. Out of nowhere, he hears a peal of distant laughter penetrating the commotion of the heavy rain. Tracing the direction, amid the low visibility, he finds Dipika in the classroom window staring at him. He wipes his eyes vigorously, *is this a dream or what*? He pinches his arm and pulls the strand of his hair to validate, indeed it is a reality manifesting like an ethereal dream. Dipika is smiling at him cloaked in spotless grace and elegance. It was her laughter a while ago that seized his attention. They gaze at each other for a long moment, a moment frozen in time, a moment to savor, like the best part of the movie, like the eloquent phrase of the poem. Dipak's cheeks sprouts into a bright smile, beaming and shining like never before. A shift of seismic proportion is transpiring inside him, his heart turning warm and light, his lifeless face glinting, his senses swear within, *that is the most enchanting smile he has ever come across.*

No matter if she harbors a feeling for him or not, no matter if it is a yes or no, no matter if it is heartbreak or heart mend, what matters is Dipika smiled at him as Adarsha had articulated, her smile is an event in itself, indeed more alluring than a full moon.

TWO

THE GIRL FROM THE FUTURE

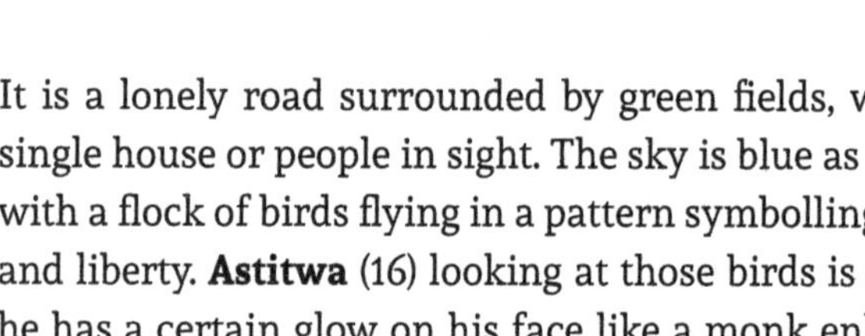

It is a lonely road surrounded by green fields, with not a single house or people in sight. The sky is blue as the ocean with a flock of birds flying in a pattern symbolling freedom and liberty. **Astitwa** (16) looking at those birds is sprinting, he has a certain glow on his face like a monk enlightened. Wearing a running gear, his biceps muscles and especially those toned legs were a sight to behold, a perfect dream body to say the least. His steps are not slowing down, his breathing in total control, not a single drop of sweat, his body motion resembling a poetic form of athleticism. Sunrises from the mountains and its rays drop on his face, its warmth slowly enters every pore of his body making him smile at the moment. Suddenly, he feels a sharp pain in his heart, it gathers momentum, a kind of pain where someone is pinching every portion of your heart. He stops his run, grabs his left chest, and plunges to the road. His heart is beating rapidly, the sheer intensity of the pain numbs his whole body, and his voice dries, Astitwa lies down on the road looking at the plain blue sky. Accepting the fact that his time is up, his vision is slowly going blurry, and a drop of tear rolls down from his eye towards his cheek. The same flock of birds is passing by him; he slowly raises his hand as a gesture to reach them. His vision is now total blank and his body ice-cold, his raised arm is falling down as it is about to touch the floor, a person grabs it. Astitwa feels warmth returning through his veins, his vision getting back to normal, and he feels the pain slowly subsiding. Inhaling deep breaths, he feels an urge to see the person, he closes his eyes and musters all his strength, grabbing the person's arm and slowly rising. He opens his eyes and turns towards the person, he finds a girl of his age, she is looking at him with a warm smile. She is wearing a bright-colored kurta with her hair flying with the gentle breeze. Realizing his pain subsiding, the girl slowly loosens her grip and leaves his hand.

"Let's take a walk, shall we?" says the girl with a smile.

Astitwa nods in acceptance.

They start walking down the lonely road, the way ahead is stretched up to infinity.

"You must be wondering who I am?" the girl breaks the awkward silence taking eloquent steps ahead.

"I can run with such pace and elegance, the day this sunny and warm and now encountering a stranger who washed away all my pain, no doubt this is a dream right?" asks Astitwa.

The girl nods her head "Ya it is, a dream."

"Who are you?" Astitwa asks.

"The girl from the future." the girl answers as she pulls the strand of hair beneath her ear.

"That means we are gonna meet in the future?" Astitwa again raises another question scratching his head.

"Yes but don't ask me the date or the place, I am not aware of it." the lady replies.

Astitwa smiles and looks ahead, there is still no end to the road. He realizes a growing comfort in her presence and this eloquent world of dreams.

"How is your heart now?"

Astitwa feels his heartbeat is back to normal now and no scars of the pain a while ago.

"It's fine I don't feel any pain... wait," Astitwa cries "Now I remember, my body is in operation theatre right now for the treatment of the hole in my heart."

The girl holds her hand "You will be fine."

Astitwa regains his calm, "Will I make it?"

The girl smiles "You will live; we will meet in the future remember?"

"In reality, I am very thin and frail... I don't have these muscles..."

"It won't matter, it just won't, I will love you with utmost sincerity and devotion, you will forget all your pain, agony, and suffering" the girl replies with an assured tone.

"How will I recognize you?" Astitwa asks.

"I don't know; it is for you to figure out."

Astitwa pauses, closes his eyes, and exerts pressure on the grip of his hand holding hers.

"What are you doing?" the girl asks.

"Soon, after I wake up, your memory will be gone but I am sure to remember the warmth of your hand," Astitwa replies.

The girl smiles, "I hope to remember you as well."

Astitwa takes a deep breath, the same flock of birds is flying over the sky. They are still holding each other's hand; the sun is going down the mountains. They both stop their steps and gaze at the twilight, he realizes this is the final part of this prophetic dream. He stares at her face forcing every nook and corner of his memory lane to remember her.

"See you in the future," Astitwa says closing his eyes.

Astitwa wakes up from the dream, bedridden in the hospital bed respirating through the oxygen mask. He finds his mother sitting in the tiny little chair. His mother gets up and smiles at him.

"You made it." His mother rejoices.

Astitwa suffering his 16 years of life from heart complications, smiles back at her knowing life has offered him a second chance. His memory is wiped clean of the dream, a year passes by, and he slowly works his way into fitness and gains muscles into the frail body, determined to serve his lifelong dream of becoming a marathon runner. One routine fine morning, Astitwa is running through a jogger's park. He is gathering momentum on his speed, his calf muscles working at full capacity, his feet trip and fall, and his knees start bleeding. He cries in pain.

"Are you okay?" a female voice is heard.

Astitwa raises his head and finds a young girl offering her hand with a bright kurta and a glow on her face. He grabs her hand and slowly gets up. Their eyes meet, her eyes it's

and he finds a flock of birds flying in the sky and that hold of her hand reminds him of something his soul had experienced long very long ago. A memory evokes, like a eureka moment,

"The girl from the future." Astitwa murmurs.

THREE

THE ROAD HOME

"Will you always remember me?" Manisha asked with moist eyes fixed upon Amar.

It was summer, a perfect June summer with the full moon shined above the mountains like a polished piece of fine art. The gentle breeze of wind directed the giant spacious green paddy fields to dance along to its tune. A bunch of fireflies flew above their head almost in a shape of a crown floating up in the air like nature's self-proclamation of these love birds being tonight's King and Queen. And the sound of cricket's rhythmic chirping added background music to the scene. Amar (19) and Manisha (16) are seated under the shade of a small tree clutching each other's hands. A final moment of intimacy as Amar was moving to the city tomorrow morning for further studies. Amar took a pause after hearing her question, he stared at those fireflies, slowly raised his right hand and patiently waited for the opportunity to grab the firefly.

"Yes, I will always remember you and me were present at this moment admiring this perfect shining moon on this beautiful night, I will always remember this gentle breeze of wind talking with your silky strand of hair and yes I will remember your teary eyes holding oceans of feeling for me no matter what, it will withstand the test of time," Amar said as he opened his fist and put the firefly on Manisha's palms.

It stayed perfectly still, illuminated by golden light through its tail. The chirping of crickets grew louder so did the soothing dance of the green paddy fields with the wind.

"No matter where I will be tomorrow, I belong to you and you belong to me," Amar said with utmost sincerity in his tone and demeanour.

"And I will wait for you till eternity," Manisha affirmed, her head rested on his shoulder, slowly a tear dropped from her eye and found home in Amar's palm.

Amar opens his eyes; he is on a local bus, homebound, to his village. The time has passed by a decade, and about to turn 30 next month, he is no longer that same 19-year-old teen with a wrinkle-free smile. He has two crutches lying on the side of his seat, suffering a life-altering bike accident Amar has a steel-plated inside his right knee. His unshaven face and uncombed hair, his pale green eyes narrating the tale of his fall from grace. It took him a decade and a serious life-threatening accident to realize his grim mistake, actually, the mistake sounds like an understatement, Crime should be the correct word. He destroyed Manisha, destruction beyond repair he never came back home after tasting the colourful dish of city life. In earlier days, Amar use to call Manisha on her landline number every Saturday, staring at her photo kept in his purse every night before his consciousness slowly faded towards dreamland was his daily routine. Despite how hard he tried, he could not stop the temptation overpowering his resilience, he started smoking and slowly binged on alcohol and fell into the pit hole of disgrace. His focus dwindled as he barely cleared his higher secondary exams, that weekly call to Manisha reduced to a call in a month and later headed to the eventual path of painful death of their relationship. Working in Thamel bar as a bartender, he worked his way up to be the manager and eventual owner of it, partying all night, he had lost his count on his one night stands with fine young ladies. Sometimes, Manisha's shades of memories engrossed his thoughts, he managed to wash it off with a pack of tequila shots.

Out of desperation and reeling from the toll of waiting, Manisha made a last-ditch attempt to salvage what little remained of their relationships, she came over to the city to see Amar. One rainy evening, she rushed onto his bar holding a small glass jar, their gaze met after a gap of 8 years. Amar quickly grabbed her hand and proceeded towards the exit. Outside the bar, in the narrow alley, heavy rain mercilessly soaked them. Amar lowered his chin struggling to make eye contact while she continued staring at his green eyes to find whether it was the same eyes that shimmered in her presence.

"Go back home, you shouldn't be here," Amar rasps as the sky bursts open with the rattling thunderstorm.

Manisha remained speechless, she realized he is not the same Amar she used to know, the spark in his eyes lost in the intoxicating charm of city lights. Her relentless tears perfectly mixed with the heavy rain, she handed over the glass jar to him and walked away, his eyes took a close inspection inside the glass. There was a small black tiny figure. As he gazed more closely, he recognised, it is the same firefly he had carefully gifted on her palms. Amar felt a wildfire burning inside him, he turned towards Manisha but she slowly disappeared in the rain. The fading drenched image of her defeated steps walking away haunted him that whole night. He indulged in a drinking rampage from that day which eventually led to the fateful night of that bike accident, in his sickbed he slowly realized all the people he considered friends or an acquaintance were mere parasites who fed on his good times as no one bothered to visit or look after him at the time of despair. When he was somehow able to walk, he took a tiny wobbly step towards the washroom, stared at his face in the mirror and spitted on his reflection, the face filled with loath and disgrace. He cried relentlessly realizing he destroyed Manisha beyond repair.

The bus stops at the small station, on his home soil after a decade nostalgia hits upon him, through the way to his house, every villager takes pity on his handicapped condition but he manages to tackle it with a brave smile. As he takes slow and struggling steps with the help of crutches to Manisha's house, he takes a pause. He walks towards the door and gives a knock, there is no answer after repeated failed attempts, he reaches home. His parents embrace him with sheer intensity, Amar cries his heart out the whole day resting his head in his mother's lap. He comes to know that Manisha has turned into a school teacher and despite her parent's repeated persistence, she refused all the marriage proposals.

The same night holding the glass jar given by her, he walks to the same place where they spent their final summer night. The atmosphere is exactly the same, green paddy fields dancing with the wind, the full moon's charm not aged a bit and the cricket's chirping as usual creating an ambience. Amar sits on the same tree, and places the jar on the ground, determined in his heart he will quietly move back to city life tomorrow morning without ever showing his face again to Manisha. He had already caused her enough pain; he didn't deserve forgiveness. A group of fireflies slowly hover above his head, remembering his past memories he is unable to hold back, and his tears again overflow knowing he cannot go back and fix what he wronged in the past. Suddenly, he hears the opening of the glass jar, he finds Manisha's face shimmering in the heavenly moonlight. She catches a firefly with the utmost care, she carefully puts it inside the jar and closes the cap, . Manisha takes a seat alongside him, Amar is sitting still unable to grasp the reality of the situation with tears still flowing like monsoon rain. Manisha keeps staring at the moon, ignoring his gaze.

"I told you right, I will wait for you till eternity," Manisha says as she drops a tear on Amar's palm.

FOUR
THE GREATEST MEMORY

An evergreen classic ballad *"love will keep us alive"* by Eagles is evocating nostalgia to the otherwise plain and shallow mood of this expensive bar and restaurant. All the walls of the spacious hall are filled with ambiguous paintings and ceilings hanging onto those chandeliers glittering like gold. Every people present is engrossed in acquainting, especially a group of middle-aged men with suits, they are dominating the ambiance, the most noticeable being a man with a receding hairline, his over-the-top gestures, and lion laughter, yes more like a thundering roar. Sitting at the corner of the hall, I check the time on my mobile, it's almost *8 PM*, I gulp down the water from the large transparent glass and proceed to order a coffee to pass this long hour of waiting. With my stomach grumbling with hunger, and having gastric issues too, I loosen the tie, fold the sleeves of my shirt and take a series of a deep breaths. A decade, I am meeting her after a decade, every major shift of technology which is directly equivalent to our life happens in that decade, it's the decade that defines a generation and paves way for the younger lot, a decade is like a weighing scale where you can put the burden of your past achievements and failures and pass a verdict based on which side weighs heavier. Her name is **Sanisha,** the person I am waiting for anxiously, my school friend actually more than a friend, I adored her, the genesis of my first love and the reason behind my first official heartbreak which shook the foundation of my existence. I was a class topper, smart and punctual, treasured by the teachers, and the flag bearer of the image of an ideal boy. I can never forget that day, we were in class 7 when our teacher introduced her as the new entrant, trembling with anxiety and unable to even raise her gaze. She stammered and struggled for a minute to even pronounce her name as she had such a soft and mellow voice. A group of backbenchers giggled, my blood pressure raised and my heart desired to roar upon them, showing my rage upon their blatant act. Teacher-directed her to take a seat gesturing towards my bench as my best friend **Ayush** was absent that day, vacating space for one. She took a seat beside me and stayed still and motionless like furniture all day long. Her nonchalant eyes, those stares reminding me of a child lost in fair, so innocent and pure, tickled my young and naive heart. It was the moment I realized I had fallen for her. Slowly and eventually she opened up to me as I showered her with all my attention and helped in her studies diligently. I can never forget the day she smiled looking at me after our teacher congratulated her on her good grades in the exam, it was her quiet and moving gesture of thanking me. My chest thumped with a quaking heartbeat. If not for the loud round of applause that ensued in her achievement, I bet Sanisha, and the whole class including the teacher would have heard the reverberation of that heartbeat. As expected, Ayush was furious with me for kicking him out of the bench and favoring Sanisha but I managed to calm him down after repeatedly bowing down to touch his feet and begging for forgiveness. He understood I loved her sincerely and vowed to support me like a true friend.

As the time passed by, Sanisha grew more beautiful and desirable, confident in the surroundings though she still was that quiet and shy girl with that infectious smile. We were inseparable, constantly chatting and discussing future aims, she dreamed of traveling all over the world and I intended to earn a colossal amount of wealth to turn her dream into a reality. Nothing literally nothing in this world was more important than her, I prayed this feeling was mutual. We were now in class 10, SLC the iron gate of school life. Ayush kept pestering me to propose to her. He explained it was now or never or you will be friend-zoned forever. I knew he was talking sense, college life is bound to bring insurmountable changes, and now is the best time. *I LOVE YOU*, simple three words to pronounce but the hardest words to confess. On valentine's day, I bought a rose as suggested by Ayush, I practiced the best ways to confess million times by staring at the mirror till late at night. I was determined in my mind during the break time when everyone will be gone to the canteen, will make a silly excuse of stomach ache with a poker face and gain sympathy from Sanisha. She would caress my head, I would put the rose in her hair like a crown and say those 3 magical words proclaiming my love. With every pore of my body oozing a hope of a happy ending, what I saw when I reached the classroom changed the course of my life forever. Sanisha seated on her bench nervously while other students were standing, cheering and whistling in rhythm with a person's singing. He was **Prashant**, a pretentious and pompous yet popular boy from our class, strumming a guitar and singing the song *"Falling in love with you"* by Elvis Presley. I knew who he was singing for, every people in the room except Ayush was rooting for Prashant. Nobody noticed me like I had turned into a wall, a piece of furniture. Prashant marked the conclusion of the song with a rose in his hand and he stepped toward Sanisha.

"Will you be my valentine?" Prashant asked with bended knees and raised arm holding flower. His trembling voice reminded me of actor Shahrukh khan.

Sanisha like on the first day of the class was unable to raise her gaze, the noise of the crowd yelled at her to accept the flower. Yet I stood there silently to witness the conclusion of this catastrophe with a faint hope that she would walk away from the scene. After moments of hesitation, Sanisha grabbed the rose, Prashant jumped in excitement, and another wave of maniac whistling and yelling dominated the room. Ayush had a distressed gaze towards me. My breathing stopped, the sky had fallen over me, *if I stay here any longer I would burst like a balloon overfilled with air.* I ran away from the class without turning back, evading those cheers and noises. My mind was bursting with deafening silence, and the rush of blood and body temperature raised. I exited the gate of the school, I yelled my lungs out on the busy road with eyes full of tears. The thought of seeing Sanisha in another person's grasp angered me to no avail. A million questions were raised, *why Sanisha choose Prashant over me for that son of a b----? Did the time we spent together mean nothing to her? Did the seed of love never sow inside her heart? Were the power of my feelings and my prayers not earnest enough?* I was running away from her, from that moment which annihilated my dreams, and broke all of my illusions of love. Now to this day, I wake up every morning and run covering infinite miles until my body showers in the sweats and my lungs beg for mercy. A part of me died that day, I desired to cease my existence, erase it from history. In the aftermath, I was never the same person again, once a bright and gullible fellow, I regressed, grew grumpy and introverted, and people had to struggle to let out a word from my lip. Yes, I ignored Sanisha in every possible way, she tried to reach me several times through the telephone and stared at me with questionable eyes in every brief encounter, expressed her concern to Ayush about my obnoxious behavior but I passed over all her efforts. Any matter or gossip concerning her I refused to listen to it. I had built a wall, an unbreakable wall prepared to protect my heart from falling into the pit hole of love again. Our school officially ended with the leave for the preparation for the exam, my concentration and focus were like an untamed wild animal, impossible to control and discipline. The big revelation came the day, the result of SLC was out, she topped me in the exam by a gap of 0.50 percent, I was happy for her but disappointed for my parents so I never went to school for farewell nor met any of my friends. Ayush too gave up on the topic of Sanisha as time passed by, I only kept my focus on becoming a chartered accountant, every arrow from my bow that was released had only one aim i.e. the goal of my career.

I wake up from my past as I hear the sound of empty glass clinking, I look upfront, a beautiful and gracious lady is sitting right beside me. Sanisha even her name rings a bell inside me, she has aged gracefully, dressed in a formal attire like me, her figure intact like in her teens, especially that brown eyes still innocent and alluring. The return of my consciousness makes me realize I am already struggling to contain myself, my heartbeat rising and throat dried up.

I am unable to make eye contact; I find the cup of coffee is untouched. Another song *"Everything I do"* by Bryan Adams is playing, that trip down the memory lane took quite a while. She smiles, and I reply back with a faint smile. *What should I say now? How should I acknowledge her?*

"Hi."

"Hello," I say as a trembling voice slips through my throat. Hearing her voice after a decade felt like finding that long-lost favorite album back in the days of CD players.

"Did you have to wait long? Sorry I had a hectic day in the office." Sanisha asks adjusting the strand of hair behind her ear.

"No, I just came by." I shake my head in reply but the stale coffee on the table is telling whole another story, *my first lie of the night.*

"You haven't changed a bit, same slender physique, same facial structure, the only change is the glasses in your eyes," Sanisha says.

"Ya," I say adjusting my glasses. "You too haven't changed."

The waiter walks toward our table and handovers a menu to Sanisha. With her gaze now engrossed in turning the pages, I now had the perfect opportunity to look at her until my heart's content. *Oh Gosh!* I could stare at her all night without getting tired.

"What do you want to have?" Sanisha asks looking at me.

"Huh....," I say quickly shifting my gaze away from her and opening the menu. "I... I will have a chicken fried rice."

"A smoked chicken pizza and a glass of wine for me," Sanisha says closing the menu.

"And for you sir?" the waiter asks.

"I am good, Thank You!" I replied shaking my head.

The waiter leaves the table leaving us all alone, Sanisha is observing the surroundings, her eyes stop at the site of business class men, that balding man is continuing on his trajectory of loud gestures and equally loud voices. My heart too is making a ruckus of its own. I need to speak and break the ice. I clear my throat; she turns towards me.

"Long time no see," I say trying to sound confident.

"10 years have passed in an instant, sometimes I wish to could go back to school again," Sanisha says with her hand still clinging to that empty glass.

I nod my head in agreement.

"How are your parents?" I ask.

"They now live in Pokhara our ancestral home; I live here alone. How are Uncle and Aunty?"

"They are fine." I throw a weak smile.

"Thank you for coming tonight, Ayush was very sure of you not attending this meeting so he hesitated to give me your number. He was whining about you not seeing him even in off days but I believed you would come." Sanisha smiles.

"He is such a nuisance, always has a habit of fabricating stuff to unnecessary limit, it's just that I am busy at work these days so I didn't have time to see him." taking a pause I continue, "Thank you for setting up this meet."

The fact is I was ecstatic when she called me up today otherwise my annihilated soul would never have had the guts to approach her. I wanted to leave all my pending work and run to her but the wound she gave me a decade ago was still fresh and the pain intact. I thought about making her wait until hours and reply with a text *"Sorry let's catch up some other time."* Indeed, a vicious planto get my revenge but as expected my heart bashed this sinister thought. like a vain attempt of salvaging water from your palm, I gave up and came here an hour earlier, prior to the call time of 8 PM.

"Samar." She calls my name like in the school days, with the same mellowness, escalating the emotion inside me, I look at her.

"After school, why did you never try to meet me nor contacted me?" Sanisha asks with a serious tone in her soft voice.

The question was so simple yet the answer harbored inside me filled with years of agony and hurt, I break the eye contact and start thinking of ways to dodge the question. Meanwhile, the waiter comes with the order, I breathe a sigh of relief as he places the food carefully on our table, he pours down the wine in the glass and leaves. Sanisha proceeds to take a photo of the dish and smiles looking at it, *guess she is satisfied with her photography skills.* The smell of the fried rice enters my nostrils and travels towards my empty stomach, those intestines grumble again notifying its need. I grab the spoon and start eating, she cuts the slice of pizza and puts it on an extra plate, and directs towards my side.

"Have it,"

"Let's have it at the same time together," I reply back with some excitement in my voice.

Sanisha smiles and cuts another slice and we both put the hot fresh pizza in our mouths at the same time.

"Reminds me of school days, we used to share lunch like this and fight over a piece of a barfi," Sanisha says as she is chewing down the pizza. "Do you still like sweets as your life depended on it?"

"No, my dentist has strictly prohibited having Sweets."

The fact is I still binge over barfi though I tried really hard to abandon this habit as it reminded me of her, I failed.

My second lie of the night.

"I never got the chance to congratulate you on your achievement in SLC result, Congratulations! you deserved it," I say to continue the conversation.

"Thank you, I accept it even though it's very late, I must confess without your help it was impossible," Sanisha empties the glass of wine in one go.

Surprised by her drinking prowess, I nod my head in acceptance and we continue eating in silence.

"I heard you are doing quite well, branch manager of Nabil bank."

"It's ok," Sanisha finishes pouring the wine. "10 years more and I will retire from the job."

"Why?" I ask surprised by her proclamation.

"I will be 35 then. With enough savings, I will invest some money in the share and estate market, the rest of the money I have decided to travel. I want my life to be full of surprises and spontaneity not waste the best years working for others." Sanisha confides as she gulps another glass of wine.

I remember it always was her dream to be a free spirit and travel the world, she has not changed a bit still the same person with exlempary determination.

"Ayush told me you are earning big bucks and will soon turn a millionaire not bad Samar."

"It's not true, to be a millionaire you need to be the financial advisor to lots of big companies and I have just started my journey,"

Sanisha nods her head, after the first slice of pizza, the plate remains untouched. Her eyes are getting drunk, slightly red, and intoxicated. I wonder why is she drinking so recklessly, *has she turned alcoholic?*

"Samar you didn't answer my question?"

"Which question?" I ask trying to act innocent even though I knew exactly which question she was referring to.

"Why did you ignore me at the end of our school days, why were you so heartless, why can't I still find the warmth that I used to admire in your eyes?" Sanisha asks as she struggles to open her eyelid, her soft voice dominated by a commanding loud tone.

Those list of soul-searching questions again evokes all my senses. I sigh deeply, I knew I need to answer her right now, no chance of escape.

"I choose career over people as I realized money matters more than friends, money makes me happy so I choose to be a Chartered accountant, that's it." I finish the sentence by shrugging and then finishing the cold bland coffee. *3rd but biggest lie of my life.*

Sanisha stares at me in disbelief, her drunken eyes are courting to find the truth, I feel her gaze is piercing through my soul, am feeling fragile like a prisoner in a cell. I avoid eye contact knowing eyes don't lie.

"You have changed... changed a lot," Sanisha says in discontent.

The rice that I am chewing is stuck in my throat, she pours water on the glass and offers it to me. I drink in silence. After staring at me for a while, she calls the waiter for the bill with dismayed body language. Our reunion is at its conclusion, I proceed to open my wallet but her hand gestures me to stop, and she closes the bill with cash. The waiter leaves with a big smile, Sanisha adjusts her hair and gets up.

"Tonight I hoped of finding an answer that has bugged me since school," Sanisha walks away from me.

She is struggling with wobbly legs yet she manages to exit the hall. *She is drunk for god's sake, what am I doing staying here, you damn coward.* I run outside the hall, she is standing on the road looking for a taxi. I quickly walk to the parking lot and start my old pulsar 200, I wanted to buy a bullet but who did I had to share the back seat. The speed of the accelerator closes me towards her.

"I will drop you."

"It's fine, I will take a taxi," Sanisha says still not making eye contact.

"Please take a seat, it's late and you are drunk too."

"Just go Samar, I will be fine."

"Please... I will be a relieved man if I get to see you walking inside your house with my own eyes." I say with an affirmative tone.

Sanisha takes a seat after moments of deep pause, I start the bike again and we leave the area. The road is almost empty, a gentle breeze of cold wind is welcoming us with open hearts, and lightning in the sky with the signal of imminent rain.

"I stay in the same home," Sanisha whispers coming close to my ears.

She still lives in the same place; I knew the address as I always dropped her home after school. The distance towards her address is shortening, Sanisha is struggling to keep awake, she gently rests her head on my shoulder. Her accidental touch sends a jolt of the wave down my veins, she is sleeping like a child. I slow down the accelerator, the speed steadies and I keep my eye especially on the bumps and holes on the road as I am extra cautious in my attempt not to interrupt her peaceful sleep. But the weather had another plan, the rain starts beating us mercilessly, and the only silver lining to consider is we are almost at the fleeting distance of her home. Finally, we reach outside her house with our bodies completely soaked in the rain. She runs inside and opens the door. The past memories of watching Sanisha enter the house after waving her hands every evening freshen up once again. After switching on the light, she yells at me to come inside. I run inside and pause at the door, she quickly brings a towel for me, I open my helmet and rub the towel around my soaked body. Sanisha is drying her hair in the towel, those beautiful strands of hair turning left, right and center. *What a beautiful sight to behold.* Her sudden stare breaks the spell.

"I should go now," I say handing her the towel.

"Stay... leave after the rain slows down," Sanisha enters the living room.

She switches on the light inside and gestures for me to have a seat. I slowly walk inside and takes a seat on the sofa, she exits the room and disappears. I take a look around the room, a framed photo of her younger self with her parents is framed on the wall, and numerous academic medals and shields glitter inside the cupboard. The wall clock is showing it's almost 10 PM. I open my tie and glasses and place them on the table. Then I close my eyes and inhale the smell of the rain, the serene sound of the rainfall showers me with immense comfort as I rest my head on the sofa. Slowly, my consciousness is fading towards a dreamland, and vivid images of school life start playing around, I am running away from the school compound evading teachers and my friends. I am about to reach the exit gate but I hear a familiar voice calling me, it stops my feet instantly. As I turn back, I see Sanisha smiling at me in a school uniform, that same heartwarming smile that illuminates my soul again. I wake up from the dream, I am covered with a thin blanket. Sanisha is standing near the window facing her back with changed clothes and tied hair. Her fingers played in rhythm with the drops of condensed rain flowing in the window glass.

"Did I sleep long?" I ask her with outstretched legs.

"Half an hour to be precise." She says admiring the weather outside.

I take a deep breath, my head feels heavy like I have woken up with a hangover, I am unable to even raise my head, *what is happening to me?*

"I know you weren't honest to my question in that restaurant earlier,"

I realize it is due to the years of accumulated unexpressed and unresolved feelings, the burden of the weight of those heavy emotions, they are responsible for the numbness in my head. I knew it is time to finally confess.

"Speak Samar, it's now or never," Sanisha says as she turns back and looks toward me.

I turn at the ceiling above, and an image of her in school uniform starts projecting again like a slide show from a projector. A drop of tear falls from my left eye and rolls towards the cheek.

"Yes I lied, I waited for you an hour earlier in the restaurant, I still eat sweets like my life depends on it even after several warnings from my dentist, and am not money-hungry nor do I believe money is greater than friendship. You and Ayush are the treasure of my life and I wouldn't trade it with anything in this world." I take a deep breath and continue, "I adored you, I worshipped you Sanisha, every action, every thought, and the reason for my existence, it belongs to you. When you shared with me your traveling aspirations, I wanted to be your companion and protect you. I always prayed that our feelings were mutual."

Another drop of tear falls, this time it travels long and falls on my shoulder. Sanisha is listening to me patiently.

"Why Sanisha, why did you choose Prashant? Why didn't you think of me? I felt betrayed, a part of me died and I was never the same person again. I built a hard shell around me. I had no option other than to ignore you, I wanted to erase your memories from my mind like formatting a hard disk of a computer but I failed miserably."

Sanisha slowly walks toward me and takes a seat on the sofa.

"The Memory of you in the school uniform smiling at me, my heart has etched it permanently like a framed picture on the wall, no matter how hard I try that image of you never falls off. You will always be my greatest memory, the best one and the most painful too," I pause and take a momentary break from my erosion of words. "I love you, I love you Sanisha till the heaven bursts, this universe melts and every drop of ocean dries, my feelings for you shall remain the same until my last breath. I love you so much."

Now free from the burden of unexpressed emotions, I slowly raise my head and turn towards her. Sanisha is staring at me with a clueless face and static body.

"You got your answer now?"

Yet Sanisha maintains that static expression without any movement. I start to grow frustrated, I have poured my heart out to her yet she isn't responding, *is she testing my patience? If it is then, it is not the best time.*

"Say something dammit," I yell failing to contain those barrage of emotions.

Suddenly before I could know it, Sanisha slaps me on my face. I am temporarily blinded by the impact. As I try to grasp the situation and look at her, her lips are trembling and her eyes watery.

"Why didn't you confess it to me earlier Samar, I used to wait for you on the road endlessly, attempted millions of times to explain it to you, even corresponded a message through Ayush but you never responded. Your ignorance crippled my world and I lost the track of my life. That day when Prashant proposed to me, I was panicking and trembling with anxiety and fear. I went numb and clueless. The deafening sound of the crowd made me pick the flower unknowingly and I acted against my will. I wanted to explain it to you Samar but you never gave me a chance. I returned the rose immediately to Prashant, he begged me to keep this a secret, and I did."

I am hearing every word of her with my mouth wide open.

"I too adored you, the warmth I felt in your presence and the comfort of your company it was heavenly and divine. When I shared with you my dream, I too wished that you would be my companion. I waited these 10 years in a hope that one day you would step right in front of this door and propose to me. I even fought with my parents to stay here alone, in case you return and you will find me here. Do you know how mustered the courage to call you today? I drank wine tonight so that I could face you, to check on my emotions so that they wouldn't get the better of me. Otherwise, I dare not even smell alcohol." Sanisha says with a weak and shaky voice.

Sanisha grabs my hand with utter force, taking me by surprise.

"I didn't let Prashant or any other men come even near my shadow, no person in this universe except for you has the right to touch me," Sanisha says as her eyes are full of tears.

I pull her arm and embrace her with sheer intensity. I start crying like a child. I whine knowing my naïve mistake cost both a decade of unprecedented pain and agony. The echo of my cry vibrated far up and penetrated the dark clouds.

"Marry me Sanisha, I don't want to waste even a moment without you."

Sanisha tightens her hold signaling her intent of approval. Both embrace each other with their bodies clasped like their life depended on it, not even air could pass through. A divine hug, a blissful hold that took over 10 years to unfold. A long overdue, separated by the fault of their innocence and now together due to sheer purity of their feelings. Nothing literally nothing in this world could set them apart now. I keep weeping on her shoulder, the barrack, the wall I had built over the years collapsed, I am feeling weightless like dust in the air. Sanisha's t-shirt is completely drenched from my downpour of tears, those suppressed and accumulated tears of a decade. Her hand runs to my back, she caresses it and kisses it on my forehead affectionately. Her heavenly touch and soul enchanting kiss keep blessing me. She knows we deserve to cry our hearts out, it is our moment to lose all the burden of the past and pave way for a new beginning. It is the moment we both surrender our souls to each other, no words needed to be said nor any actions left to quantify the intensity or depth of our emotions.

A bolt of lightning strikes, but its deafening impact has no sort of effect on the strength nor grip of their hold, they are firm and at complete ease at the moment. Meanwhile, rain continues its downpour soaring with each passing minute like it has a point to prove, maybe those dark clouds conspired to warrant a happy ending for these soul mates.

Indeed, a happy ending!

FIVE

Heart War

A giant-sized colourless metal gate opens, and a guy with a dry and pale face comes through, he has messy hair with large green eyes gazing below the road. A kind of gaze which did not hold even the slightest bit of emotion nor any form of life in it like a blank book without any words. The sun hiding among the mist of the clouds breaks free and bestows its holy rays upon the earth. Rahulraises his palms to cover his eyes from the harsh lighting of the sun and turns back to a large antique house with a board titled *"Heartbreak Hotel"* that is seen behind those large metal colourless gates. Rahul takes a deep breath; he is feeling the warmth of those sun rays after a week of isolation inside the heartbreak hotel, "A place where your heart is replaced by a fully functioning artificial one, nor can you love nor your heart will be broken again". After all, it is the heart that manipulates all the human emotions, conspire with the universe to make us fall in love and waives the concept of a soulmate, it is the heart that beats for the person you have an intense fondness for, it is the heart that refuses to move on after the painful break up rekindling the feeling in every moment. Every living being on this earth is born with a certain instinct, heart's instinct is to ditch the logical prospect of life, and to never let a person forget its instinct is to love regardless of the suffering he/she bears. And heartbreak hotel facilitated to break this human suffering after a person's heart is replaced by an artificial one, he/she will lose the ability to love as the person won't have a sense of feeling or any form of emotion. The person will have all the memories of his past and present intact but it won't generate any kind of reaction or sentiments like a robot that person will be free from all the barriers of feelings and attachments, and will only understand the logical prospect of life like a heartless person. Rahul recently broke up with his long term girlfriend and it was the endgame for him.

"Rahul, we have to end this relationship, my heart is not with you anymore," Sneha said after Rahul wished her a happy new year staring at the full moon.

My heart is not with you anymore...that phrase fired like a bullet and assassinated his heart, Rahul lost his sense of balance from that night. From losing his banker job to losing his sanity, his parents could not bear the sight of their son's situation. No amount of counselling from his psychiatrist or suggestions from his family helped a bit, face soaked with tears his thoughts only rewinding the moments spent with Sneha. To put it precisely, this was a setback so catastrophic, a pain so deep rattling every sense of his body, Rahul's heart still refusing to acknowledge the fact that his soulmate moved on. Despite million requests from his parents he opted to get a heart transplant as he felt he won't survive even a minute let alone the whole life, he needed to get rid of this numbing pain which shattered him to the core. After spending a week in heartbreak hotel, completing the formality of the operation, his heart was finally swapped with an artificial one. Now walking outside the gate, Rahul feels no burden of his traumatic memories of Sneha like a huge weight has been lifted off his chest, all the past events again playback in his consciousness like an edited film without garnering a single ting of feeling inside him, his mind taking the control with rational thoughts as the artificial heart's task is pumping blood to all the vital organs of the body not to create an emotional ruckus anymore. A bus stops near him, Rahul enters and takes a sit, there are many people inside who are returning to their destination like him all losing their battle against the emotion called love and opting for exchange of their hearts. The bus starts moving along the road surrounded by forest, and the filtered oxygen from the thousand trees breeze through the window of the bus. Filling his lungs with the fresh air, Rahul tucks his palm inside his t-shirt and feels the mark of the surgery on his left chest. Reaffirming the decision that he took a week ago, a thought crosses his mind he will never fall in love again and no longer this heart will beat for someone ever, he is a free spirit now.

Rahul's Parents embraces him with full intensity after reaching home, both have eyes filled with tears but he feels no sense of emotion, he just stares back standing still like a portrait. Days turn into night, the warmth of the spring makes way for the chill of the winter, Rahul is surviving his life diligently performing all his duties of son and an office employee, his life all sorted out now like in perfect order without the distraction of emotions and sentiments. His parents and friends lost account of the time they last seen him smile or grabbed by any form of melancholy. Showing pictures of his childhood, and friends narrating good old memories, nothing helped in garnering a reaction from him, Rahul only had that feelingless face with lifeless eyes every day every moment. Even when he encountered Sneha in the busy street of Thamel, he just passed by her like a gust of wind, with no more tears or scars of the past.

On an annual trip with his banking colleague, they are at the snowy mountains of kalinchowk, the place is looking like a giant winter land with heavy snowfall covering all the grounds. Rahul is standing outside the hotel wearing a large brown winter coat staring at the sky-touching mountains while his friends are grabbing snow in their fist and hitting each other. Their constant screaming and laughing in sheer excitement doesn't affect him as he is only feeling the harsh coldness of the weather ignoring the call of his compatriots to join them in the fun. Suddenly, a ball of snow hits his left chest, he falls to the ground, a peculiar pain runs through his chest extending to the heart, breathing heavily, looking at the misty sky, a cotton like snow falls on his face. A secure hand grabs by his arms and lifts him,

"I am sorry.... I didn't mean to hit you; I was playing with my friends."

A lady wearing a winter cap and a thick woollen jacket is staring at him with an anxiety-filled gaze, a certain warmth light's up to his whole body, that accidental snow hit and the touch of the lady wakes up the part of his subconscious that was lying dormant after the surgery. Staring into her eyes, Rahul feels a tingling sensation inside which slowly translates into a heartbeat picking up pace rapidly.

"Are you ok... please say something?" the lady says wiping the cotton-like snow from Rahul's face.

Her touch sends his every sense fluttering, Rahul presses his throbbing left chest, he cannot believe this is happening again, he thought his heart won't beat again for someone, the warmth of someone's presence won't be felt again, this strange kind of feeling won't be experienced again in this lifetime, not with an artificial heart but it all proved wrong.

"Please say something?" the lady asks again without breaking the eye contact.

"I... I am fine." Rahul replies looking into her eyes.

She breathes a sigh of relief and smiles showing her braces and helping him stand on his feet. It starts snowing, she again smiles and opens her gloves to feel the fresh snow, small wrinkle forms in Rahul's cheeks, which slowly translates into a weak smile and his eyes fill with newfound life. Like it was written in the stars, the law of nature shunning all the logic even a manmade heart won't stand a chance against the power of emotion, that artificial organ eventually felt the human sentiments. Looking at the snow-filled palms of the lady, it is the moment Samar realizes it is not about the silly tiny heart but an instinct of a human race, the instinct to surrender in the conspiracy of the universe's magical moment and fall in love again. They both keep walking in the snowfall ignoring the call of their friends and colleagues.

SIX

THE STUBBLE

The cool breeze of wind and early Rays of the sun caressing the cheeks of **Preeya** (22) revealing a small mole on the left side of her upper lips, a thought is constantly crossing her mind "**Hesitation leads to consequences**". Riding the scooter in her comforting pajama, she has a sense of rush and sheer determination in her gaze, she is wearing a misfit slipper beneath with a speed of over 60 km per hour fully optimizing the intensity of her feeling. It's a 7 AM Saturday morning, and the road is empty and without traffic, she realizes a piece of half-chewed sandwich stuck inside her left jaw, she quickly gulps it down her throat.

She had dumped **Sujan** a month ago, the irony or you may say it a plain simple coincidence, they had started dating on the 1 day of 2020 i.e. 1 January of 2020 and she broke up with him on February 1st. So the number one connection was the common point between the blossoming and fading scenario of their infant relationship. She liked Sujan, he had this uncanny ability to make her laugh until every part of her cheek muscles stretched to its limit and started hurting. A freelance writer by profession, he was a loner and an introvert every limited thought and words he expressed were like a gem, profound yet incisive like a flowing river that knows its ultimate destiny is to meet the sea. Preeya felt immense solace in his presence like her heart found a permanent address to rest, she thoroughly enjoyed listening to his fiction-based stories and the part where he always complimented the small mole on the left side of her upper lips, she literally blushed every time. The only problem or nuisance she felt was his untidy hygiene habits. Despite her insistence, Sujan always procrastinated the habit of shaving his stubble and always wore that single pair of black converse he owned, Preeya detested the feeling of the sting on her cheeks from his stubble while they were hugging each other. She always felt the sensation of thousand bees stinging her face. After bidding goodbye, she always checked her face in the rear mirror of her scooter whether she has gotten any rashes on her cheeks from Sujan's stubble. She had visited his single rented room and it was a complete mess, unpleasant smell with unmade bed, and clothes were haphazardly thrown in every corner of the space, it was the final nail in the coffin for Preeya. After months of persuasion, she finally listened to her best friend and agreed to meet prince charming that perfectly matched her classic taste. That night Preeya head off straight to Sujan's room and told "I am leaving you".

"I had a feeling it was going to happen soon". without turning back in a slow and assuring tone "even if there is a 5 percent chance of you returning back to me in this lifetime I am going to count on that chance and be hopeful, I never thought I could date a girl as beautiful as you. Thank you Preeya". Sujan answers with a valiant smile.

Indeed, the guy she met afterward was a charmer, with inch-perfect parted hair, and a clean-shaven look oozing confidence through every pore of his body. It was a cloud nine experience for Preeya as his every move fluttered her heart making her truly believe the idea of the perfect match does exist. They hugged before departing, Preeya ecstatic inside for the fact that his neat face didn't sting even a slight bit. Preeya slept with a magical feeling inside her stomach that night, the shades of Sujan slowly fading away from her memories. The magical touch didn't last long enough, she realized a feeling of emptiness growing inside every day. Once a charming talker, his every word and demeanor started to feel way too immaculate, like a perfectly programmed robot with equally perfect capability. Slowly His clever one-liners failed to elicit even a weak smile, neither his stories nor incidents were fascinating enough. His hugs turned colder day by day, something was missing something very wrong, she expected that her life will turn for good and be a bed of roses but she was left with the aftermath of profound emptiness. Her working productivity was getting affected, she had stopped interacting with her colleagues and stopped taking the call of a so-called perfect match. Until today i.e. the Saturday morning, her mother forced her to get up early for a routine family breakfast get-together. Her mother baked pancakes and prepared some grilled chicken sandwiches. Her favorite pancake tasted like plain water, moving that sunken cheeks she is forcefully chewing struggling with every bite. As she takes a bite of the sandwich she notices a cut on her father's clean shaved chin. Like a eureka moment, yes it's that stubble, the stingy sensation of that Sujan's stubble, the touch that she loathed in the past was the prime thing that she was missing all these days. The misty scenario in her consciousness clears up, she realizes she had almost committed an offense by breaking up with Sujan. A person need not be perfect, what matters most is how you feel when you are in presence of that person and yes she felt at ease and deep comfort in his company. Preeya quickly gets up and leaves the breakfast table, her mother questions her call. She quickly answers "hesitation leads to consequences". Her father smiles and tells his wife he was the one to preach this thought to preeya.

She is right outside her house Sujan, Checking her face in the rear mirror with guilt-ridden eyes she curses her past choices, she parks her Scooty down the road without bothering to open the helmet. She quickly starts climbing the staircases, every step pumping her heartbeat almost giving a feeling that her heart will burst wide open. The only thought that is ringing in her mind is the warm hug of Sujan with the stingy sensation of his stubble. Finally, she is on the third floor, taking a deep satisfying breath she turns the knob, the door open as Sujan has a habit of not locking the door. She enters inside, and the outlook of the room has a 360-degree shift from the last time she saw it. Sweet room freshener is dominating the air and new bed sheets with no sign of clothes lying here and there. A single drop of tear falls from her left eye suddenly she hears a voice of a male humming a tune coming from inside the washroom. She walks towards it; she opens the door. Sujan hanging a towel on his shoulder is about to shave with his face filled with shaving cream. The shaving blade is about to clean through those stubbles.

With huge bulging eyes gazing at Sujan, Peeya shouts with all her might "No".

SEVEN

Spotless Smile

I never smile nor laugh, I am unaware whether is it a genetic defect or those funny bones inside me are yet to develop and nurture. My mother (widow) narrates to me that once she woke up in the middle of the night to a loud noise of a person giggling, upon inspection she found out that it was me who was laughing with sheer intensity in my sleep, she had to sprinkle water on my face to wake me up. I was six back then now I am 25, that historic event took place 19 years ago with no memory of that dream which tickled my funny bones. I have seen people laugh out loud up to the point where drops of tears are flowing freely, in inspiration I have tried reading funny jokes, listened to countless comedian's instances, visited several doctors, and had multiple people tickle those hard ribs all those efforts turned to be a colossal failure. My adulthood relentlessly pressures my consciousness to apprehend the social norms and present a weak smile in front of people but I fail, my facial muscle refuses to take the command it forbids and acts on its stubbornness. So this is a very peculiar case of me, nothing heard of before I guess, and yes I smoke too, each and every object in my room has the nasty smell of the cigarette, and sometimes I feel those nicotine has replaced my reproductive body cells, simply I live to smoke. **Sangu,** she is my adorable girlfriend, I love her with utmost sincerity and dedication, I feel heaven has showered me with a beautiful gift under this eternal blue sky with her gracious presence. Shealways pulled my cheeks out wide, my facial muscle stretched up to the point where a forceful smile took shape, it opened up the cave of my mouth revealing those teeth tarnished by the habit of my chain-smoking. That is her routine nature to greet me, I hate it but still, I know it makes her happy and I am ok with it. She also tops the list of the people who had numerous failed attempts in webbing a smile on my face. We roam around the city in her classic blue Vespa, enjoy the city lights view from the top of a hill, and walk nonchalantly without any fixed destination, she can talk tirelessly while I listen without losing a bit, and we get drenched in the rain every monsoon and take a sip of tea with extra sugar to soothe our sweet taste buds. She sometimes shares my smoke but coughs it all out, I pat her back playfully to which she smiles with red teary eyes and at that moment I really wish I could smile back. Her existence has tamed my restless soul, I could embrace death without any fear such was the comfort of her hold when she hugged me and when the warmth of her lips touched mine, I evaporated like water, my body obliterated and turned into dust entering the realm of her galaxy, every being of me became hers.

I am waiting for Sangu under the shade of an old single tree hill, the sky is covered with clouds all over paving way for the monsoon, it could turn people to forget once sky used to be blue. I always try not to smoke in her presence and here I am already struggling to contain the fetish to inhale that tobacco-filled nicotine. There she is, cool like a cucumber, she parks her scooter and starts walking above the way of the hill as I am at the top, I have eyes on her every move. I have combed my hair inch perfectly with a gel to which she never failed to complement and reassure, I again rearrange my hair with an old plastic comb once used by my later father. Sangu closes the proximity, I can look at her properly, she is stunningly dressed in a white t and blue jeans. But something is different today as I closely inspect every part of her body, I realize it's her eyes, sleepless, her lowly stare is devoid of any life. She passes me a weak smile but her arms remain firm, with no intention to pull my cheeks, a single sweat runs through my forehead towards the cheek. I anticipate those words to be spoken but it's the silence that is descending, like a calm before the storm. Sangu is refusing the eye contact, I could see her hands trembling and feel her invisible breathing. She runs her hand into her purse and takes out a passport, she starts turning pages, and she stops and sighs. Sangu shows me the page where there is a stamp of approval i.e. a visa from Australia. Suddenly, an airplane flies above us in unusually close proximity, the deafening sound reverberates the whole surrounding and a rumbling quake beneath the ground. Her hair hovering wildly with the wind, *I wish I could run my fingers through her hair and fix it.* Yet I stay still as I am frozen, I am staggering due to the aftermath of the revelation. I am unable to bear the weight of my feelings, my head turns downwards, I always thought Sangu will always be beside me under the eternal blue sky, alas what a silly belief I had. There is a faint sound of sobbing, *Is Sangu crying or am I hearing things, why can't I bloody move?* With trembling feet, I gather all my strengths and I raise my head. She is wearing a black goggle, a perfect camouflage to conceal her emotions, my pale blue face is reflecting through its dark glasses. She hands me over her Vespa key and turns back without uttering a single word, she takes some hesitant step forward, and my heart skips a beat with a belief that she will turn back to me, shedding those sunglasses and grace me the opportunity to look at those eyes one last time. She pauses for a bit, I stretch my neck to analyze her body language but this time her feet quickly move with conviction and before I could know it, she is already walking her way down the hillside. I am sweating profusely and my stare refuses to blink, it keeps soaking the final twilight image of her. Sangu is gone without any explanation raising a million questions inside me and I am here, still and erect like a statue, immobile and lifeless.

Separation is hard to digest but the hardest part is to learn to live in that person's absence. I wake up with that heavy feeling, if I manage to smile in some way or another, she will not be witness to that spectacle. It has been raining since the day she left, riding her gifted Vespa, I roam the city alone, everything seems weathered, every nook and alley, the roads we use to walk painted by her memory now stings me like a cactus, vivid night city lights have turned into a colorless fest and that tea tastes like plain water. My chain-smoking has escalated to new heights, now I smoke two cigarettes in a single take, earlier the stuff in my room used to have the nasty odor of cigarettes, and now every pore of my skin emits nicotine. I stay on the single tree hill all day long, soaked in the rain, counting the number of the planes that take flight and waving to each one in her remembrance. With my gaze fixed on the tree for countless hours, I have developed a sense of relationship with it, it is my confidant and I believe that in the past someone like me who couldn't bear the departure of his soulmate turned into this sad little tree. Someday in the near future, I too will turn into a solitary tree and be a source of solace for others.

Days keep passing by, rain is not slowing down nor showing any signs of its eventual conclusion, it's like dark clouds have plotted sinister revenge to cease the existence of the blue sky. My story too must find its conclusion sooner or later, lost in thoughts about riding the Vespa, drenched completely from top to bottom, I stop and park it below the single tree hill. My body is feverish with each and every joint of my bones in severe pain yet only with the help of my sheer will, do I climb my way up to the steep hill. With every precise step matching the drops of the rain I reach the top, withstanding the relentless weather. Breathing heavily, I am struggling to even stand properly, my wobbly legs are about to give up, if this is the end of my journey today, looking at the sky I pray to let me turn into a tree. *Will and spirits waning and accepting my fate, I am about to close my eyes and drift towards an eternal sleep.* With my blurry vision I turn towards the single tree, in a surprising turn of events, a person is standing there holding a transparent white umbrella and that pink gumboot standing out. My whole body is charged up with euphoria of hope, *could it be Sangu? Did she realize her mistake and come back for me?* To seek an answer, I concentrate on my fading awareness towards uncovering the persona beneath the umbrella, I take my slow steps towards the tree. With a rising heartbeat and building anticipation, I am preparing to approach the person unguarded. Under the shade of the tree, standing like a portrait without any slightest movement, I raise my hand and knock on the umbrella. As the umbrella slowly raises upwards sprinkling water over my face, a beautiful yet desolate face is revealed, no she is not Sangu yet I am not filled with the obvious disappointment. With shoulder-length wavy hair, and a mole right at the middle of their eyebrows, her stare is casting the spell on me, she has a distinctive aura like a godsend savior in this doomed weather. I am standing still, losing the perception of time, she turns her gaze and breaks the stare which for a while felt like an unbreakable vow. I silence my mouth as I thought words could ruin this tranquillity, we both stand below the tree as a complete strangers without expressing each other's motives.

I light a cigarette to warm up my soaked body, blowing the smoke and seeing it disappear amid the rain is giving me strange solace. I offer her a smoke without hesitation, she brainstorms for a moment without any changes in her expression. But eventually picks a piece and puts it in her mouth. Slowly my trembling hands holding that lighter ignites the fire staring at those luscious lips. As she deeply inhales a puff, she coughs severely, and the cigarette drops on the ground, I hold the umbrella and immediately run my hands through her back, patting her with utmost care as I did to Sangu. Her cough slows down, she rubs the tears from her eyes and sighs. I am staring at her, running her finger through her hair she turns toward me, and our stares meet again, this time a smile forms on her face, a heart-warming one reminding me of a child, angelic and pure. My rustic heart is melting, opening the door of my dormant subconscious as a movement of seismic size is happening inside me. With my face getting warmer, cheek muscles stretching automatically, mouth opened wide, and body quivering rapidly. I realize it is late but it has already manifested, the surrounding is echoing with a roar. It is of a loud laugh, guffaw, a long overdue, a wait of 19 years, like an angel breaking the spell of an evil witch, this lady did what Sangu and my entire acquaintance only hoped of, this stranger made me laugh, an uncontrollable one indeed.

She too is smiling back at me, a spotless smile growing with each passing moment. The rain is slowing down conjuring a hope for the blue sky, my eyes are getting teary and my body is exhausted. *Yet, I am feeling a deep comfort in her presence and my miracle laugh's echo is escalating and reverberating in the whole atmosphere.*

EIGHT

CHATTEL

It is spring, a small hill is surrounded by an unknown breed of flowers each petal Separate in color, red, green, blue, yellow you could have forgotten the count, like a colorful marriage of flowers its sheer beauty and outlandish diversity mesmerizing beyond words. A surreal sight to behold like a garden gifted by nature. The sky is peculiarly blue as if a painter with divine abilities proceeded to paint it, the clouds look like a roll of cotton balls, and the green grass on the ground is laid across like a carpet. The aura of stillness and tranquillity of the place breaks as an incoming footstep is heard, and a slender built girl with heavy breathing enters the frame. Geetwearing a grey oversized bomber jacket with mustard-colored classic converse at the feet, she has a pale yet elegant face which defined epitome of sadness, a face without room for joy remindingwithered charm of the autumn season. She has big alluring eyes with sheer depth that gave a feeling of holding oceans of secrets inside. Geet takes a pause and stares at those enchanting flowers, it elicits no reaction in her facial muscles may be déjà vu struck upon her or the beauty of those mystifying flowers failed to charm her. Her demeanor signals she is familiar with the place, and her breathing slowly returns to normal, she opens the oversized jacket and lies down maintaining some inches of distance from the bunch of flowers. Geet carefully places the jacket at the gap between her and the flower, stretching both arms under the carpet-looking grasses. She rests her head and turns towards the jacket, slowly raises her arms, and caresses it with the utmost care, she pulls one arm of the jacket towards her and places it on her chest covering both shoulders. It is clear, that it is an act explaining her imaginative state, sketching an image of the hold of the jacket to a hold of a beloved person. Geet takes a deep breath, tiredness grows into her perfectly still face. She grasps the arms of the jacket placed on her shoulder tightly and slowly closes her eyelids, like a projector in a dark room, a montage of memories of her past starts to play into her slowly fading consciousness.

It was during that lazy winter, that she encountered a person that altered the course of her life, always a shy and nonchalant introvert character Geet never imagined falling for a person to put it simply he took her heart and soul. Always a light sleeper, frequently waking up every night due to the loud snore of her father, one morning she decided to take a walk after her mind refused to shut down due to the constant snoring fest. Walking across a narrow path surrounded by green fields, the morning sun is rising from the mountains with a flock of birds flying in the sky. Appreciating the grace of nature, Geet finds a tall guy coming from the other side wearing a hoodie. She lowers her gaze and continues moving, they come close, only inches apart as the space is very narrow she stops her feet in order to find space for both to pass. She moves towards her left, the guy moves towards his right blocking the passage, and quickly Geet moves to her right, the guy follows to his left creating an awkward situation as both are stuck in the middle of a rice field. All the while, she has her eyes on the floor unable to muster the courage to make eye contact. Both standing idle at that moment, she gets a smell of his fresh breath as he blows a deep air out of his lungs before she could even realize it, she gets a quick smooch on her cheek. The warm contact of his lips on her skin jolts shocking waves, her face and especially ears turn red she touches her cheeks and raises her chin. There he is standing tall like an imperishable mountain, his spotless face glowing, bathing in the sun like a divine presence, covering his head with the cap of the hoodie, staring at her with a smitten look. Geet is gasping for air, before her mind goes numb and trips over she closes her eyes. Slowly, catching over her breathing, filling her lungs with the fresh breeze of the air, she opens her eyes, the guy is gone nowhere to be seen.

That entire day she thought about the guy stirring her fingers on her red cheek, his audacity to kiss her in the first encounter which illuminated her entire senses, the warmth of his lips intact and the smell of his breath fresh, most eventful his face that non-compromising intense stare of him which shook her entire foundation. One thing was for sure he had a mysterious aura about him, like a lost soul searching for answers, she again wakes up in the morning and walks the same path to see him. With misty thoughts prevailing in her mind, she finds him on the same narrow path surrounded by the fields, he gives a puny smile with a confident gaze as if he had the premonition of her arrival, and he starts walking ahead. Like a magnet attracting a metal, her feet start moving on their own following him through the fields up to the way towards a hill without sharing a word in total silence. The road is steep and rough,

Geet having lost idea of the miles she had traveled, she is breathing heavily and struggling with tired wobbly legs while the guy is walking without any fuss.

"I am tired... I cannot go on." Geet is struggling to maintain her breathing.

The guy turns back and comes closer with a calm demeanor, he points his finger towards the hill.

"It's the best place on the entire earth, someday you will be ready and reach there," The guy says.

From that day their meeting thickens as Geet had her winter break from college they stayed under the warmth of the sun all day without speaking, walked miles and miles sometimes brushing their shoulder accidentally. She found solace in his presence like a sense of telepathic understanding, not a single word needed to be spent. Every moment in his presence was a soul enchanting experience, she never felt the urge to ask his name, identity, or family background nor did he bothers to explain it to her. He always wore classic vintage jackets with a pair of black converse and she loved how he always smiled to greet her.

It was new year's Eve night, only minutes left for midnight they are walking the road towards her home. Suddenly, a thunderstorm is heard, Geet startles with the deafening impact of the sound.

"Do you have a secret?" The guy asks with a calm gaze at her eyes.

"I don't have any," Geet replies struggling to maintain eye contact as his stare always pierced through her soul.

Small drops of rain start falling over them.

"Wait... I will tell you mine." The guy smiles.

He quickly moves towards the middle of the road, closes his eyes, and stretches his whole body. Slowly, he moves his shoulder in a rhythm followed by his hands and legs soon it turns out to be a perfectly synced dance move with the beat of raindrops. Geet could only stare in admiration of his dancing spectacle.

"I like to dance in the rain that's my secret."

The guy closes in and holds her hand, a rush of blood hits her brain. In the chill of December, they start walking ignoring the rain, a set of fireworks flash in the sky brightening up the darkness and signaling the welcome of the new year.

"We will go to the hill tomorrow and this time we will reach there." The guy says looking at the fireworks.

Geet nods in acceptance, the warmth of his hold protecting her from the harsh weather. She could walk all night without bothering about the rain, the freezing temperature, the soaked clothes, and hair, or the fatigue as long as his presence is guaranteed. The next day, they start their journey tough towards the hill dominated by a small forest knowing it is a daylong hike, Geet chooses to wear a thin sweater. Step by step, this time determined to reach the top of the hill she musters all her strength and walks in sync with him without taking any breaks. The steep path of the forest tests her physical will enormously but Geet passes through all the barriers walking hand in hand with him and finally reaching the top of the hill. The surreal garden of colorful flowers with the carpet of soft grasses welcomes them, Geet is Spellbound almost in tears by the sight, each petal with separate colors, stuff only available in dreams. The guy rests down and smiles.

"I told you right... this is the best place on earth."

A blow of wind whistles past her, her hair floats in the air, and she takes a seat. They stay still admiring the view, the breeze of cold wind is gathering momentum.

"Is this place real?" Geet asks breaking the silence.

“It is.... those flowers never fade they stay the same in every season," The guy answers, "You want to ask anything about me?” He asks staring at her eyes.

“Why did you kiss me in our first encounter?” Geet asks as her body is shivering with the freezing wind.

He quickly opens his grey bomber jacket and carefully places it on her shoulder covering her body. Geet feels the warmth returning to her senses.

“I don’t know, I felt I should and I don’t regret it.” The guy answers with an endearing blush.

The honesty in his response comforts her soul, Geet rests her head on his shoulders, the amenity of the moment, the tranquil vibes of the place eases her mind, this is a place where she wanted to be all her life with a person with whom she finally found solace. Slowly, she closes her eyes and drifts towards sleep.

And that was the last she saw of him, he disappeared without any goodbyes, no reasons to explain, he was Gone with the Wind just like that. Wearing the jacket given by him, she regularly walked the same way, same alley, same narrow path of the rice field, where they first met in a hope of seeing him with no success. She waited for him in the same place all day long every day skipping college, soaked relentlessly in the rain at the road where he shared his secret. The feeling of suffocation hit her hard like her soul longing for the other half, every moment without his presence brought her an insufferable agony. Still, she never loosed hope and clung to that grey oversized jacket as if her life depended on it, it became her pillow at night, her style statement, and she carefully washed it every week. Slowly. time passes by the warmth in the air returns with the arrival of the spring season, and the never-ending wait for him takes its toll on Geet. The candle of hope slowly faded, crying every night to sleep brainstorming for the reasons for his disappearance, she wished to see him once, no matter the price she had to pay or the consequences she had to bear, it had to be him no one else. And one fine day Geet took the decision to again walk towards the surreal hill where they last met.

Geet wakes up from the series of flashbacks now back to reality, the blue sky is surrounded by dark clouds and accompanied by the violent wind. She gets up, the jacket is gone, moment before she drifted towards her nostalgic past, she knew she held that jacket with her all her might creating zero possibility of it being blown away by the wind. The surreal flowers are dancing in rhythm with the strong breeze, white cotton clouds turn into a menacing dark mist, the whole surroundings turn into a gloomy fest, and there is shattering noise of the thunderstorm. A scary scenario manifested, first she lost that jacket, and now the weather showed no mercy upon her. Before she realizes it, her eyes are filled with tears knowing there is no use in staying, she turns around to return. But her feet freeze immediately, the sight ahead paralyzes her existence. Amid the dark and gloomy murky view ahead, she finds a silhouette figure wearing that same jacket standing some meter's distance ahead.

Slowly, a smile takes shape on that weathered face of Geet.

NINE

Lost Stars

Solitude, Dipti craved solitude, days of peace, nonchalant, lonesome time. It recharged her exhausted fidgety mind after periodic socializing, long hours of interaction with people sucked the energy out of her, draining her physical and mental attributes. Though she has always been an extrovert, the spirit of the party, unabashed with a quirky sense of humor, she never confided in anyone that some quality alone time shrouded in stillness and composure, was her cure, a bliss. *She chose to keep it a well-guarded secret as a convenience.* Sultry air greets her as she opens the window, the climate is quite hot tonight with the temperature soaring above 30 degrees. Dipti loathed the sound of AC so she never turned it on. Her jaded face with equally famished eyes, the secluded hotel room with a large attached unmade bed and plain lifeless walls, pin-drop silence pointed towards the fact she is indeed in a solitude. The irony being she did not choose it, unforeseen, unprecedented circumstances imposed this isolation upon her. *She tested Covid positive two weeks ago*, experiencing discomfort around her chest with a sore throat. Being a responsible person, she was immediately quarantined in a hotel room. Fortunately, none of her family members got infected. *When something that a person craves gets to acquire in abundance then that something loses its value,* this stretched 14 days period of solitude too was turning into an insipid fest, the monotonous and tedious routine turning her sullen and grumpy. Like a punishment of imprisonment, she could order anything, contact anyone, nestle on the bed endlessly but without the license to step out. Restricted freedom, was the catalyst, the genesis of her frustration. *Her mother's warm presence, her father's loud yet rhythmic snores, her crush's infatuating smile, and a long satisfying puff of a cigarette.* She was missing them all, the longing for social interaction escalating with each passing moment, peaking the level of her discontent.

There is a knock on the door, *twice*, signaling the dinner has arrived. She opens the door, spreading her long desirable legs in a short, blessed with tall height and lean frame, and picks the dinner packet below the floor. Dipti takes a sniff, but no luck, her sense of smell still up for a toss, she stares at the long empty corridor. On the top floor of the hotel designated for quarantine, she feels that the silent, overstretched, narrow corridor is mocking her loneliness. As she takes the step back to return, a scene halts her movement. Another packet of dinner is expected to be picked up, it is below the door adjacent to her room. *Room number 555,* She reads it twice, her room number is 556. *555 .... I am quite intrigued by the number,* Dipti murmurs. Amid the chaos of isolation and recovery, she never bothered to pay attention to her room number, let alone others. She decides to wait, even a brief interaction with the stranger in the room shall be worth it. The vintage wall clock's heavy pin is moving at a brisk pace, a minute and a half pass, the dinner packet still abandoned. A curiosity escalates, a fervent desire and her feet freeze on the floor with rapid-fire questions. *Who could be the owner of the packet? More importantly, who is the one residing in room 555, that thought never crossed before where numerous person is residing on the top floor quarantined, reflecting and drowning in the depth of their loneliness, same as her feeling miserable.* Driven by her impulsiveness, she slowly closes her ears towards the door, attempting to eavesdrop. Yet, there is no hint of noise, perfectly quiet and composed. She takes a deep breath, distances away, and stands still like furniture wondering the reasons for the delay. In a swift moment, that dormant room 555 opens, a hand clutches the package and the door is shut, *BAAM*. It manifested so sudden, passed too quickly for her eyes to read and recognize, *like a whisk of air, impossible to anticipate and predict.* Dipti sighs deeply and enters her room with mixed emotions, every thought burdening with the failed pursuit of encountering the owner of the room. *Gee... what was I thinking eavesdropping into that door*? An *invasion of privacy, a punishable act, ah... too many thoughts... fuck.*

Dipti tries to shrug it off by opening the food packet, she had ordered a hamburger with fries, growing tired of having a so-called healthy diet for a speedy recovery. She consumes the food, obviously without any sense of taste. Back in the home after dinner, she cunningly sneaked out to the terrace for a quick smoke. That last cigarette dated two weeks ago which almost felt like a century now. Dreaming of those liberating nights, she enters the washroom. A long stare at the toothbrush, she holds it close.

"Thank you for serving me well, you're the only thing will remember about this insipid room." Dipti chats with her toothbrush.

Dipti sanitizes her hands and slips to bed, her laptop still logged in with an unfinished season of *End of the f**king world on Netflix.* Finger's crossed that if tomorrow's report is negative, she shall be granted freedom, to escape from this quarantine. *Pointing their middle finger to the virus in her imagination as an act of wrath for all her sufferings,* she unlocks her mobile for some social feed.

"How was your day?" A text from her crush *Shirish.*

"Wish you were here." Dipti types the sentence and deletes it instantly. Instead, she taps on an emoji with a smile, "Holding on, awaiting tomorrow's test results" and sends it. They accidentally met at a mutual friend's birthday bash, his reticent personality attracted her. Throughout the whole time, he rarely talked, a perfect listener and observer. Before departing at the gate, Shirish timidly asked "I forgot your name?" Dipti was startled at that moment, utterly speechless, a rare occurrence like witnessing a meteor shower, nobody in this universe had the ability to enamor her. Yet, she grasped into her senses and told her name. Shirish nodded his head and just walked away, no waving of hands or announcement of his departure. Her ears turned tomato red, face burned, eyes blushed, feet fumbled and heart leaped towards stars with the surge of unchained emotions. *He spoke with his eyes, Dipti realized in that brief conversation.* Her thoughts take a back seat as she hears a knock on the door, it's past 8:30 PM.

"Who is it?" Dipti asks.

No answer.

"Who is it?" Dipti asks again.

Was her ear ringing? Did she imagine the door knock? Another curiosity escalates, leaving the comfort of the bed, she opens the door. No one, all room doors shut, and that long corridor still mocking her loneliness. *Cursing her impaired hearing or whatever it was,* she proceeds to enter her room. Just then, the door unlocks, it is room 555. Dipti slowly turns, the door is half opened, *through the narrow gap, in the dim view, she is able to see half face of a person staring at her. Almost like a silhouette figure,* the poor lighting inside that room is hindering the visibility, impossible for Dipti to analyze that stranger's face.

"Hello," Dipti says in an impulsive reaction.

There is no reply. An awkward silence ensues; even in low light that stranger's eyes are gleaming, round in shape, and filled with depth staring at Dipti without break. That lips zipped passing the verdict, no words shall escape from it.

"Hi there." Dipti again greets in the hope the stranger will reply.

"Hello." The stranger replies after a long period of waiting.

It is a voice exuding eloquence and calmness, a kind of voice that can soothe a fidgety and restless mind, just a single word made a sheer impact on her, *it is a voice of a lady.*

"I am Dipti." Dipti introduces herself in a bid to prolong the conversation.

"And I am Sandhya.... My first day here." Sandhya says in the same calming tone.

"And it could be my last night here.... If tomorrow's result is negative." Dipti says crossing her fingers.

"Oh.... I hope it is." Sandhya replies slightly distancing away from the door.

Ignoring the dim view, Dipti now could figure out Sandhya has a perfectly symmetrical face shape like an engineer designed with impeccable measurement supported by short shoulder-length hair. *They are now 5 and a half feet apart precisely.* The door still half-open, perhaps

Sandhya felt secure in concealing her appearance.

"I hope you too recover soon," Dipti says to comfort her.

Another awkward silence, a moment where Dipti has so many things to talk about but silly words failing her spectacularly. *Tick Tock* of vintage wall clock is dominating the ambiance, signaling 9:00 PM.

"Did you have dinner?" Dipti asks.

"Just swallowed it," Sandhya says exhaling deeply.

"Me too, my sense of taste is still out in a prolonged holiday, no hope of immediate return," Dipti says sarcastically.

No response from Sandhya, the ball is on Dipti's court, she has to be the instigator otherwise the conversation won't last long.

"Do you have all the symptoms?" Dipti asks.

"No, just sore throat and loss of taste."

"Do you smoke?" Dipti bites her lips, *that's not a question you should be asking in the first conversation, slip of a tongue. Should she apologize? Her impulsiveness again about to land her in trouble.*

"Yes."

"Do you have a cigarette?" Dipti asks quickly with a hopeful gaze.

"Yes, but..."

"Can you give me one?" Dipti interrupts her in excitement.

"I only have one left; need to savor it for later."

Dipti groans loudly in disappointment, her hope of a smoke shatters. *Fuck, covid again.*

"Sorry wish I could have shared it with you." Sandhya expresses her apology.

"It's fine, how often do you smoke?" Dipti asks shrugging off the disappointment.

"Only at night after everyone is asleep, seated on the window ledge of my room and in the company of cool summer breeze," Sandhya explains her preference.

"Wow, same here, the only difference is I sneak into the terrace and sometimes I steal one from my father's packet," Dipti says with the excitement in her eyes apparent.

"I find solace in that burning cigarette," Sandhya replies back to back without any delay.

"And I just enjoy how I am able to manipulate the intensity of smoke that exits through my lips, deep and long, short and brief depending on my mood," Dipti says.

"That fading smoke leaving a trail of our existence, evaporating towards the wilderness of the universe." Sandhya expresses a thought slowly opening up to Dipti.

Fading smoke leaving a trail of our existence.... Dipti takes a moment to admire the profundity of her thoughts, she just enjoyed smoking never was her consciousness grasped with deep sentiments towards a tobacco-filled injurious cigarette.

"The first thing I will do tomorrow is to have a hearty smoke, my heart and soul are cravings for a cigarette, health protocol of Covid can go to hell." Dipti expresses her frustrations.

Now the silence in between didn't feel awkward anymore, who would have predicted a topic of cigarettes would connect two strangers in a spiritual way.

"Actually I saw you earlier standing as I picked up the dinner packet," Sandhya says hesitatingly.

"Oh..."

"After shutting the door, I realized I should have initiated a conversation so later I knocked on your room, guessing it was yours." Sandhya finishes the sentence.

"I am glad you did," Dipti affirms with a smile.

"Actually I had..." Sandhya sighs deeply and abruptly stops.

Dipti is able to notice some cracks, underlying tensions in her voice, and *sharp contrast in the calmer tone from the beginning.*

"It's ok." Dipti smiles.

"No, it's not." Sandhya's voice is turning vulnerable

"I am sorry if I said anything wrong, I am really sorry."

Sandhya remains quiet, her heavy breathing dominating the ambiance.

"I had a panic attack earlier. Anxiety hit me so hard that like a maniac I went out of my room and knocked on your door. I was in desperate need of some human contact but then I realized, my actions could have its repercussion so I ran back." Sandhya confesses out of nowhere.

That confession leaves Dipti staggering, she never thought a person with such a lilting, soothing voice had a mental disorder. She had friends and colleagues who only had confided about their bad days in the office or troubled relationships but never expressed one's mental issues. She remembers some advice, read in an online forum, the most important thing to consider while helping an emotionally distressed person "*What not to speak is more important than what you are about to say.*" Asking wrong questions, and passing judgemental views will only aggravate the situation.

"I understand. Please..." Dipti gets interrupted.

"Sitting idle all day inside the room, I succumbed to a fear that I will forever be imprisoned inside this hotel room, I felt the walls were closing, succumbing and suffocating me."

Sandhya closes the door, her left hand clutching the edge. *Her long fingers with fresh scratch scars towards the nail fold are visible.*

"So easy for them to explain relax, control your mind, it's just a thought, look at the people outside struggling for a morsel to eat, and here you are privileged, yet a wimp, " Sandhya continues, "Why can't they bloody understand, it's not easy, hardship is not only defined by physical struggle, there are a bunch of people like me who are struggling psychologically, every day is a challenge it's like surviving in the abyss of darkness, crippling under the burden of your own thoughts, living like a prisoner, you can neither run nor plot an escape when the nemesis is your own mind, mind that is a never-ending war zone." Sandhya finishes the rant with the rage in her voice apparent, her grip tightens on the door.

Dipti takes a deep breath and opens her lips to speak, just then.

"It's so hard to even breathe.... Everything was hard to even before, now this quarantine is wreaking havoc on my weak and fragile mental health." Sandhya exclaims.

Dipti wished to hold on to her hand and console her but the safety protocol wouldn't allow so. Sandhya's emotions are running wild, on a rampage. She needs to calm her down, *the conundrum was from where should or how should she start?*

"Thank you for confiding in me, it takes a lot of courage and bravery to express bottled up, suppressed emotions," Dipti takes a pause and continues, "I empathize with all your sentiments, mental health is as important as physical wellbeing," Dipti says raising her hand towards the heart.

"If x-ray machines could also detect fractured thoughts then articulating about mental health would have been so easy."

"I feel you Sandhya, peace of mind is vital for everyone. Nothing is more important than that."

"It's such a frightening prospect that I have to live all my life alone with these fears."

"Take some deep breaths, it helps."

Dipti can hear her slow long gradual breathing.

"Can I ask you a question?" Dipti asks.

"Yes."

"Have you taken professional help?" Dipti asks.

"No, I loathe the term mentally ill or a mental patient, I panic with the thought of people around the clinic staring at me in sympathy. I want to selfheal and I hope to selfheal not depend on the medications." Sandhya expresses her concern.

"Hope is the most powerful emotion; I believe it has the strength to move mountains. The fact that you are nurturing such beautiful feeling, I know that hope will blossom into a garden of strength and peace."

"Just need someone who will listen to all my troubled thoughts without any of their niggling advice and sympathies." Sandhya expresses her concern.

"Advice that's the only thing people offer without cost, pretending to be an enlightened Guru."

"Sometimes it's just not about advice, it is about a person's voice getting a platform to be heard," Sandhya adds.

"Exactly, just sit back and hear it without any preconceived notion. It really means a lot to have someone like that."

"Can I ask you another question?" Dipti asks.

"Yes."

"How did this all started, your problems?"

"I can't recall, I was very sensitive since I grasped over my consciousness," Sandhya sighs, "I feel emotions too deeply, I think my mental issues are the repercussion of overthinking and knack of being too sentimental."

"That means you are special; this world is full of plastic people without any sense of emotions."

"My parents always try to downplay the extent of my problem rather than understanding it." Sandhya takes a deep breath and continues, "The problem is the people I considered friends, they pissed me off with their insensitivity and ignorance."

"You know what I do when people piss me off?" Dipti questions.

"What?" Sandhya asks.

"I have a punching bag inside my room, imagining that person's face, I punch with rage till every part of my muscle is exhausted."

Sandhya chuckles.

"It helps, really. Try it." Dipti giggles.

"Sorry I am still conversing in the dark, I feel shy and apprehensive about my appearance, So...."

"No it's fine, however, you are comfortable, that is more important." Dipti says, "I think one should ignore the circumstances that are beyond our reach or control, focusing on regret rather than redemption is the root of our problem."

Sandhya exudes a *muffled hmm...*

"In the darkest moment of your life, I need you to focus on the gratitude aspect of life, think about the wonderful family you inherited, those unfulfilled dreams, some wonderful friends we made, and bid goodbye, the moment when realized someone loves you unconditionally, your first kiss," Dipti says winking her eye.

Sandhya remains silent.

"The sheer joy of your parents watching your first baby steps, your first nonchalant smile, and the first word that escaped from your mouth. Now they may not understand your issues like the way you expect but at the end of the day, they never gave up on you and neither should you." Dipti explains calmly.

Sandhya is still silent but her breathing is now steady and her body language composed.

"What is your best memory? In a sense the most treasured moment of your life?" Dipti raises a question.

"I can't recall," Sandhya says.

"Me too." Dipti continues, "Sorry I am acting like an enlightened one right now. Please excuse my preachy words."

"No, in fact, I am feeling better now." Sandhya slowly removes her hand from the door.

"Thank God!" Dipti says.

"Actually all the things I told you earlier, are like fruits of realizations I managed to harvest in these 2 weeks of isolation, some bitter, some sweet and sour. Family, they matter the most, nothing else does more and nothing ever will." Dipti says with sheer honesty.

Sandhya nods her head, "Thank You."

"Thanks to you too, every day I was agitated by the circumstances. I am now at peace and proud of this sense of realization bearing into me."

"You seem so easygoing, I bet everyone loves being around and you never had to face mental barriers." Sandhya questions.

"I am a jolly person and popular in my group. I have always been the life of the party." Dipti smiles.

"As I expected."

"Amid all these years of growing up, I am realizing that I never tried to accept my real self." Dipti takes a deep sigh.

"I don't understand." Sandhya questions again.

Dipti remains silent for a moment.

"I conceal a side of me which I have not confessed with anyone so far." Dipti continues.

Sandhya's silence is subtle approval for her to know it's time to confess.

"I enjoy solitude, even though I act extrovert but I am ambivert by heart, social interactions take a toll on me. I crave and need isolation in order to recharge. Out of fear of being tagged a loner and getting cornered by my friends, I chose to keep it a secret." Dipti confesses.

"But real friends won't corner you know your real self. They will embrace it." Sandhya says.

"I know that I succumbed to the pretentious flashy world, for the sake of pleasing others, the void in me kept growing deeper."

Dipti sighs deeply again, "See you are not alone in this world drowning in fear."

Sandhya nods her head.

"Now I am not afraid nor ashamed of it, I don't care if my friends will understand it or not, I choose to accept solitude with open arms."

"You decided the right thing."

"You gave me the courage, otherwise I wouldn't have..." Dipti continues, "Or maybe I hadn't found a confidant until now." Dipti says staring at her.

"The moment we started our conversation, I felt secure, a feeling blossomed that I could trust you," Sandhya says.

"I am honored.... you know I have never had this profound conversation even with my closest of friends."

"I too don't remember being this expressive about my emotions."

"Now I am starting to wish this was my first day.... We could have a conversation like every day." Dipti complains.

"Ya... but I think that is the most special part, you will probably leave tomorrow and we will both have something worth remembering every day, this limited yet profound conversation, a beautiful memory of tonight," Sandhya explains.

The vintage clock points it's past 9:55 PM now.

"I think we should go to bed now," Sandhya says.

"Yes, we should." Dipti agrees to gaze at the old clock.

Both stare at each other silently, before departing.

"You know what?" Dipti asks.

"What?" Sandhya asks curiously.

"I want you to meet me after you are done kicking ass of COVID alright?"

"Ok," Sandhya says nodding her head.

"If you don't..." Dipti takes an abrupt pause.

Sandhya is waiting patiently for her to finish the sentence.

"If you don't, I will track you, will hide in the bedroom closet, and surprise you," Dipti says in an authoritative tone.

Sandhya slowly disappears in the dim view, and Dipti feels astonished.

"Sandhya...." Dipti calls her.

No answer.

After a moment of uncertainty, Sandhya walks back towards the door.

"We will share this last cigarette together. I will save it for our reunion." Sandhya forwards the last cigarette she owns.

Dipti smiles staring at her thoughtful gesture.

"And we will leave the trail of our existence from the fading smoke in this wild, wild universe." Dipti humors repeating Sandhya's thought a while ago.

Sandhya chuckles.

In fact, that chuckle grows into a laugh, unchained, liberated laughter reminding her emotions for the time being unshackled, free from anxiety, overthinking, and every mental barrier. Dipti joins her with a loud guffaw.

One by one, each door of that corridor opens simultaneously, every quarantined people visibly shaken by that clamorous laughter of Dipti and Sandhya. *That desolate long corridor sprouts into a new life, it looks lively and exuberant.* **The door of room 555 opens completely, and** the light switches on, Sandhya is standing 5 and a half feet apart in the gleaming fluorescent light. Dipti is now able to anatomize her face without any visibility issues. Sandhya's exposed appearance evokes a familiar yet dormant feeling inside Dipti.

Every ounce of her presence reminds Dipti of a long-lost friend and a lifelong confidant.

TEN

A Fresh Start

Osin is standing at the side of the road near her apartment with piles of disposable items wrapped inside carton boxes, she has a pale face as if a smile hasn't resided since eternity. Accompanied by her friend Muna, she is staring at the box filled with items of personal belongings which included a teddy bear, greeting cards, packets of ribbon-wrapped chocolates, and a grey apron with shades of red pigment at the top of the pile. A chef by profession she washed that apron several times but that obstinate red stain refused to fade away like her tenacious heart refused to wash away memories of him. Osin was left reeling after she separated from her long-term boyfriend due to irreconcilable differences, it took her months of psychiatrist sessions, therapy meditations, and million sheets of napkins to tame her free-flowing tears. After a considerable amount of persuasion from Muna, she chose to migrate to a new apartment. A constant war between her heart and mind resulted in a resolution of dumping all his belongings and decluttering all his remembrances. That grey apron was gifted by him and that red pigment was a result of cooking a spicy dish which he was always fond of, always wearing it while doing kitchen chores, that apron became a part of her body, a slice of her existence.

Osin mustering all her energy and strength picks up the carton box and tosses it into the large garbage one by one, she feels as if her heart is about to jump off her chest realizing it is easy to throw stale old items but the not the ones with an emotional worth. As Muna puts her hand around Osin's shoulder, she takes a deep breath and reminds herself this is done and dusted finally parting from his memories. She is looking outside at the trash can while her friend Muna is preparing lemonade to wash away the hangover of the previous night. A garbage truck stops by, Muna hands her the glass of lemonade and rests on the sofa.

"You did it Osin... this is your fresh start," Muna says caressing her temple.

Osin remains silent gazing outside, two men open the trash can and toss the carton boxes at the back of the truck. Her whole senses start freezing, those men were not dumping trash but dumping a part of her soul leaving her in oblivion. The men get inside the truck, it slowly starts moving away.

"A fresh start." Osin mumurs.

Out of nowhere, she finds a familiar face running towards the truck as the misty scenario clears up it is him whose memory runs through her veins. An emotional upheaval reaches its peak, the glass of lemonade falls from her hand and crashes on the floor, she quickly moves out of the apartment and follows him through the road, the truck is way ahead still the guy is pursuing him relentlessly. Osin getting out of breath manages to close on him.

"Akash," Osin yells with all her might.

Akash stops and turns back, wearing a leather jacket with classic blue jeans he looked nothing short of an idol. Osin feels as if she is looking at him after ages, he walks up to her without breaking eye contact, and soon only some inches of distance separates them.

"They took away our memories," Akash says struggling to maintain his breathing.

Osin is overwhelmed by the moment as she realizes she was not only the one to bear the heavyweight burden of this split, the love of his life Akash too felt the same way, the soul-wrenching agony, endless tears and longing for a second chance. Akash is staring at her with longing eyes, he opens his mouth to speak but she interrupts.

"Let's have a fresh start," Osin confesses.

ELEVEN

CAMOFLOGAE

It is Five past five AM, and that vintage clock tower at the end of the street is standing tall like an imperishable mountain, it is still dark sunlight yet to grace the humans with its holy rays. It had rained relentlessly last night complimented by earth-shattering thunderstorms, wild wind conjuring a feeling of an inevitable apocalypse. The wrath of nature helped wash away the filth of the town which could be considered a silver lining in disguise. A man in his mid-twenties opens the shutter of his floral shop, checking himself out in the small mirror on the wall, and stands still at the counter, staring out the window with an awaited gaze.

Tiny drops of rain are falling freely on a pothole of mud water, footsteps on it, and a huge splash dominate the once tranquil ambiance. Through the illumination of street light, that anonymous figure is gleaming holding a colorful umbrella resembling a perfect rainbow with an oversized yellow raincoat and a pink gumboot without the revelation of the face concealed beneath the horizon of the spacious umbrella. At a constant nonchalant pace, enters the floral shop, the guy inside smiles wholeheartedly, quickly grabs a bouquet of lilies, and hands it to her. The umbrella perfectly masks its face the only visible part being those hands with long graceful fingers with grey nail polish, without missing a beat grabs the flower, puts the money at the table and walks away from him. A routine had formed for the floral shop owner as every morning at 5, that mysterious person walked in and grabbed flowers without exchange of any words. He had several failed attempts to interact and peek at the concealed face but all he could say was the long dark hair, blink and miss the view of those luscious alluring red lips confirming the person to be a fine young lady. Those feelings of curiosity gradually planted a seed of compassion and fondness for that umbrella-holding enigma, his consciousness sketched a surreal image of her persona in his heart, this morning determined to follow her in a hopeful revelation of her face in return. He grabs his jacket, cautiously closes the shutter, and moves his feet towards her walking ahead, he cunningly manages to maintain distance without getting noticed.

They pass through various quiet deserted streets and reach a secluded side of the town. With the minty smell of wet birches, a cemetery is in sight, she is walking ahead crushing the dry leaves scattered around enters, he stops his movement and hides behind the thin wall to observe her actions. The umbrella enigma walks around for a bit and settles at a grave with the name of John Fernandez, she drops the umbrella, the early rays of the sun kiss her face, glittering long dark hair with a side profile of her face is revealed, her eyes completely closed the most noticeable feature being her lips and the pointy nose. His heart skips a beat, awaiting dearly for this moment of revelation, all his senses prepared to finally gaze at her face, like a destiny to be fulfilled his feet start moving on their own. She replaces the wet stale flower on the grave with the fresh bouquet of lily and raises her both hands to pray. As he is moving towards her, a hand tightly clasps his shoulder from behind, he turns back, and finds a middle-aged lady with a pale exhausted face and pointy nose staring at him, he gasps at her abrupt presence. The lady shook her head vigorously, bewildered by her mannerism he is unable to grasp her encoded form of communication. Finally, she opens her mouth to speak

"Do not disturb... She always sleepwalks at the dawn of the morning to mourn for her lover." The lady murmurs.

Printed by Libri Plureos GmbH in Hamburg,
Germany

9 798887 040141